Dear
Lincoln,

I can still remember like
the day you were born like
it was yesterday! We were
so very excited and filled with
love and joy! You are an amazing
little boy and I we wish you the very oops!
best first birthday ever! You are the best little ~~monster~~ monster around!.

♡ Zia Carli, Zio Charlie
+ baby Elliott
xoxo

THIS MONSTER NEEDS A HAIRCUT

WORDS & PICTURES by: bethany bARTon

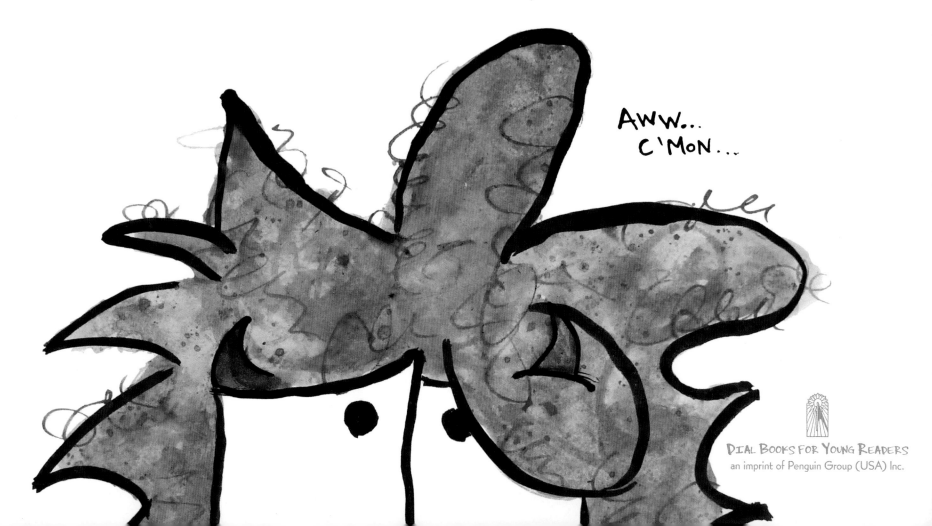

AWW...
C'MON...

DIAL BOOKS FOR YOUNG READERS
an imprint of Penguin Group (USA) Inc.

THIS BOOK IS DEDICATED TO:
MY PARENTS, FOR TELLING ME TO DREAM IT
MY HUSBAND, FOR TEACHING ME TO WORK FOR IT
& MY AGENT, FOR ASKING ME TO SHARE IT

DIAL BOOKS FOR YOUNG READERS
A division of Penguin Young Readers Group • Published by The Penguin Group • Penguin Group (USA) Inc., 375 Hudson Street, New York, NY 10014, U.S.A.
Penguin Group (Canada), 90 Eglinton Avenue East, Suite 700, Toronto, Ontario, Canada M4P 2Y3 (a division of Pearson Penguin Canada Inc.) • Penguin Books Ltd, 80 Strand, London WC2R 0RL, England
Penguin Ireland, 25 St. Stephen's Green, Dublin 2, Ireland (a division of Penguin Books Ltd) • Penguin Group (Australia), 250 Camberwell Road, Camberwell, Victoria 3124, Australia (a division of Pearson Australia Group Pty Ltd)
Penguin Books India Pvt Ltd, 11 Community Centre, Panchsheel Park, New Delhi - 110 017, India • Penguin Group (NZ), 67 Apollo Drive, Rosedale, Auckland 0632, New Zealand (a division of Pearson New Zealand Ltd)
Penguin Books (South Africa) (Pty) Ltd, 24 Sturdee Avenue, Rosebank, Johannesburg 2196, South Africa • Penguin Books Ltd, Registered Offices: 80 Strand, London WC2R 0RL, England

Designed by Bethany Barton and Jennifer Kelly • Typography by Bethany Barton
Manufactured in Singapore on acid-free paper

1 3 5 7 9 10 8 6 4 2

Library of Congress Cataloging-in-Publication Data
Barton, Bethany, date.
This monster needs a haircut / by Bethany Barton.   p. cm.
Summary: Stewart's parents think he needs his first haircut but he refuses because his hair is perfect for collecting spiders and hiding treats, until it grows so long that it interferes with his favorite activity—scaring.
ISBN 978-0-8037-3733-4 (hardcover) • [1. Haircutting—Fiction. 2. Monsters—Fiction. 3. Humorous stories.] I. Title.
PZ7.B28465Thi 2012   [E]—dc23   2011029972

The artwork in this book was created using Higgins inks on paper & perfected in Photoshop.

LIKE SCARING ANIMALS AT the ZOO.

ROAR!

AND PRACTICING AT THE FIRE-BREATHING RANGE.

AND COLLECTING SPIDERS AND...

"Hi, Stewart!"

THAT'S FELIZ, SHE'S STEWART'S BEST FRIEND. SHE LIKES ALL THE THINGS THAT STEWART LIKES:

PAINTING

READING

Sometimes Stewart's Hair Gets in the Way...

ESPECIALLY WHEN HE "FORGETS" TO BRUSH IT ...

FOR DAYS...

WEEKS...

OR EVEN MONTHS.

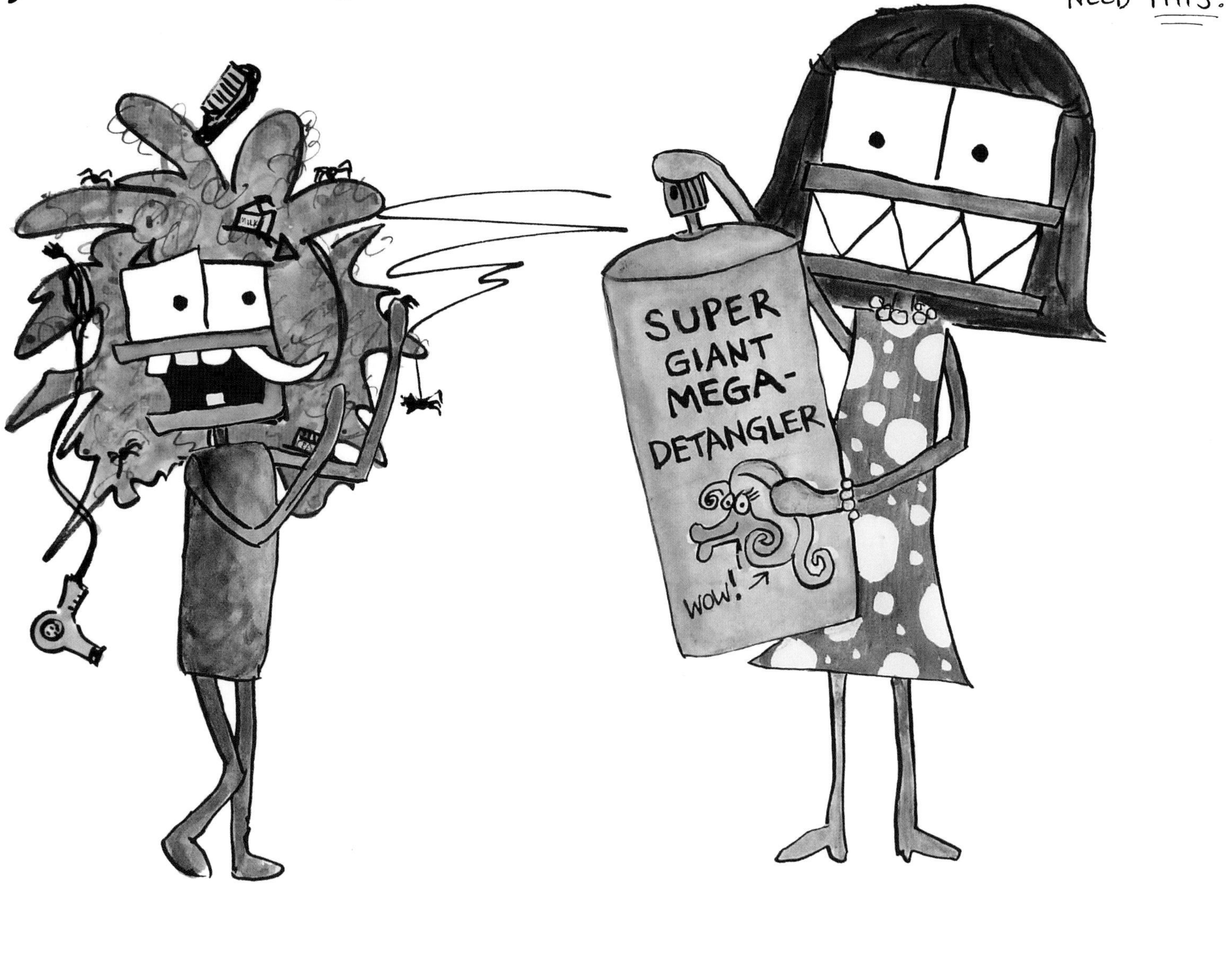

STEWART'S DAD HAS THE PERFECT SOLUTION:

HAIRCUT

STEWART'S DAD
CAN BE A LITTLE
DRAMATIC SOMETIMES.

HIS HAIR IS TOTALLY HELPFUL FOR MONSTER THINGS!

LIKE CASTING SUPER-SCARY SHADOWS.

AND BLENDING IN WITH SHRUBBERY AT NIGHT
(FOR SURPRISE SCARING).

AND WHAT IF IT NEVER GROWS BACK?

WHERE WOULD WE KEEP TOYS AND TREATS FOR AFTER SCHOOL?

CRAYONS

NO... A HAIRCUT SIMPLY WON'T DO.

MR. GREGO'S CLASS

Rory Snarls

Grimington Grime

Jessica Ressa

Graham Hogan

Monster Steve

Ruckus McGee

Bridget Hurry

Sloth Jr.

Smashley Growl

THE NEXT MORNING, STEWART'S DAD HAD SOMETHING TO SHOW HIM.

THAT'S ME AT YOUR AGE!

I WAS THE FIRST MONSTER IN SCHOOL TO SUCCESSFULLY SCARE A GIRAFFE (THEY DON'T SCARE EASILY).

STEWART'S DAD WASN'T GETTING IT.

SO STEWART CAME
UP WITH A PLAN.

DEAR DAD,
THANK YOU FOR
SHARING THE
COOL OLD PICTURES.
YOU TAUGHT ME
HOW TO SCARE A
GIRAFFE WHEN I
WAS A BABY, SO
I DON'T THINK
I NEED A
            HAIRCUT.
I LIKE MYSELF
JUST THE WAY
I AM.
THANKS, DAD.

SINCERELY,
STEWART

HMMM...
CAN'T ARGUE
WITH THAT.

AND LIFE WENT BACK TO NORMAL FOR A WHILE.
WELL, NORMAL FOR STEWART.

AND STEWART'S HAIR JUST KEPT
GROWING AND GROWING ...

AND GROWING!

SOMETIMES THINGS
GOT LOST IN THERE...

(EVEN IMPORTANT THINGS).

FELIZ'S
GLASSES

HOMEWORK

DAD'S KEYS

weeee!

BUT THAT DIDN'T STOP STEWART!
SOMETHING ELSE DID.

STEWART'S DAD SHOWED HIM FUNNY
PICTURES OF HAIRCUTS HE COULD GET.

HE EVEN TRIPLE-PROMISED
STEWART'S HAIR WOULD GROW BACK.

SO STEWART DECIDED
GETTING A HAIRCUT
MIGHT NOT BE
THE WORST THING IN
THE WORLD.

BUT THE NEXT MORNING, StEWART WAS FEELING A LITTLE SHEEPISH ABOUT HIS NEW LOOK.

LAMPSHADE

CARDBOARD BOX

BASEBALL CAP

ROAR!

WELL... MAYBE NOT ALL THE WAY BACK.

"I LOVE IT!"
FELIZ SAID.

"IT'S THE PERFECT SCARE-CUT!"

THIS IS STEWART.
HE'S A MONSTER.

← He HAS HORNS.

AND NOT-SO-WILD,
NOT-SO-MESSY,
PERFECT-FOR-SCARING
HAIR!